D1625342

Dog Watch

BOOK SIX

The Turtle-Hatching Mystery

By Mary Casanova
Illustrated by Omar Rayyan

Aladdin Paperbacks
New York London Toronto Sydney

This book is a work of fiction. Any references to historical events, real people, or real locales are used fictitiously. Other names, characters, places, and incidents are the product of the author's imagination, and any resemblance to actual events or locales or persons, living or dead, is entirely coincidental.

ALADDIN PAPERBACKS
An imprint of Simon & Schuster Children's Publishing Division
1230 Avenue of the Americas, New York, NY 10020
Text copyright © 2008 by Mary Casanova
Illustrations copyright © 2008 by Omar Rayyan
All rights reserved, including the right of reproduction
in whole or in part in any form.
ALADDIN PAPERBACKS and related logo are registered
trademarks of Simon & Schuster, Inc.
Designed by Tom Daly
The text of this book was set in Gazette.
Manufactured in the United States of America
First Aladdin Paperbacks edition January 2008
2 4 6 8 10 9 7 5 3 1
Library of Congress Control Number 2007929325
ISBN-13: 978-1-4169-4783-7
ISBN-10: 1-4169-4783-3

Dedicated to

the dogs of Ranier, Minnesota—
past, present, and future

And

to Kate, Eric, and Charlie—
and to our family dogs, who have
brought us tears and trouble,
laughter and love
over the years

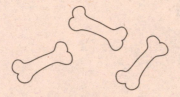

True:

On the edge of a vast northern Minnesota lake sits a quiet little village where dogs are allowed to roam free. Free, that is, until they get in trouble. One report of a tipped garbage can, nonstop barking, or car chasing and the village clerk thumbs through *DOGGY MUG SHOTS*, identifies the dog from its photo, and places a round sticker on the culprit's page. Then she phones the dog's owner. Too many stickers and the troublesome dog is ordered to stay home—tethered to a chain or locked in its yard. No more roaming, no more adventures with the other dogs of the village.

Leaving Home

"Criminy biscuits!" Chester said from his dog crate in the belly of the plane. "I still can't believe our owners are taking us along to Mexico!"

"I don't know," Kito replied. "I'd rather have my paws on solid ground back in Pembrook." Crated across from Chester—along with other unfortunate cats and dogs—his stomach went up and down with every bump. Everything ahead was uncertain. He was heading to a whole different country with all new sights, sounds, and smells. And if there was one thing he didn't handle well, it was the unknown—especially *strangers*. He imagined Mr. and Mrs. Hollinghorst somewhere else in the plane, probably in comfortable seats, sipping coffee. He'd give anything to be at home in Pembrook, where everything was familiar. At least there he knew what to expect.

"But think of it!" Chester agreed. "A whole seven days of vacation!"

"A hot vacation," Kito said. His thick chow chow coat trapped in heat and made summers in Minnesota miserable. He couldn't imagine heading farther south!

"Kito, we'll lie around in the shade. Nap. Eat. I mean, ever since Dog Watch started, when have we taken a break? Keeping Pembrook safe is a good thing, but it's a lot of work!"

"True," Kito agreed. "Dog Watch means constant *vigilance*."

Nearby, Schmitty, their black Labrador pal, woke up from his nap with a snort. He apparently wasn't the least bothered by winging his way somewhere above the clouds. He chimed in.

"*Vigi*-what?" Schmitty asked, with a shake of his black silky ears.

"*Vigilance,*" Kito repeated. "It means, well, keeping a constant lookout and never letting up. Keeping Pembrook safe at all times requires vigilance."

"Yup," Schmitty agreed. "And that's why I'm ready for a vacation! Wahoo! Soon as we get there, I'm hitting the ocean!"

"That's right," Chester agreed. "Long strolls on the beaches at sunset. Hanging out with our owners . . ."

"Begging for snacks," Schmitty added wistfully.

Kito heaved a sigh. "I don't know. Once a Dog Watch member, always a Dog Watch member. But how do we do our job in a new place? We don't understand the language. And we won't have our Alpha dog with us." He thought of Tundra, their alpha dog who kept the dogs in order at home. "I mean, I worry that Tundra and the other dogs are

3

going to need us. We should be back home, not heading out on vacation."

"Blazin' beagles!" Chester said. "You worry too much. Do you even know the word 'vacation,' Kito? It means re-lax-ing."

The plane lurched, and the three dogs flattened in their crates. For several minutes, the plane jolted, grumbled, rumbled, and shook with turbulence. Kito squeezed his eyes shut. A cat meowed miserably. If the plane fell from the sky, there wasn't a single thing he could do to stop it. He swallowed hard, waiting for the worst. Then, just as quickly as it had started, the plane settled back into a calm and steady drone.

When the other dogs started chatting again, Kito fell asleep. But when the plane wheels lowered with a loud *ka-thunk*, he nearly jumped out of his amber coat and bonked his head on the crate's roof. Then the plane roared like the dragons he'd read about back home when the Hollinghorsts and Chester were fast asleep, of course. Though he'd learned to read as a puppy, it was a talent he kept secret. As the plane bumped along unsteadily and finally slowed to a complete stop, Kito felt dizzy and a little sick to his stomach.

At baggage claim, Mr. H proclaimed, "There's our boys!" Leash ready, he opened up Chester's crate.

"See?" Mrs. H said, opening Kito's door, attaching a leash, and letting him out. He stretched his head down to the tips of his paws to ease his knotted stomach and legs. "That wasn't so bad, was it, Kito?"

"Huh, easy for you to say," he said, but of course she couldn't understand him. Only dogs could hear the language of other dogs. If they met other dogs in Mexico, would they speak the same silent language?

Kito glanced at Schmitty's owner. A wide-brimmed green hat covered Hillary Rothchild's pale skin and black, coiled braid. She leashed Schmitty, and then the owners and the three dogs headed outside the terminal to a waiting van.

The curb was hotter than Pembrook's

pavement in July. Kito's paws heated up fast. In the steamy air, his coat's thick under-layer and overcoat began to warm. He wished he could cool his paws in the cold lake waters of Pembrook. He'd rather be at the fire hydrant with the other dogs, sharing the latest news, or solving a new mystery.

"What a pretty dog!" exclaimed a woman in bright gold sandals. She stepped closer and closer to Kito. He backed up toward the van.

"Oh, it takes him a little time to warm up," Mrs. H said, coming to his rescue. But the woman kept coming.

Kito crawled under the van.

"Sorry," the woman said, turning and walking away.

Kito inched back toward Mrs. H. People of all sorts, shapes, and sizes bustled in and out of the airport. They poured in and out of cabs, vans, and buses. This was going to be a whole week away in a new place—with new faces, strangers—everywhere he turned. His fur bristled.

"C'mon, Kito," Mrs. H said with a smile as bright as the floral shirt she wore. "We're finally here! Mexico! You're going to have fun!"

Tail between his legs, Kito jumped reluctantly into the van. All he wanted was to go home!

Danger in Mexico

The van driver lifted his sunglasses from his eyes, glanced in the rearview mirror, and asked, *"Español?"*

"No, sorry," Mrs. H replied. "We speak only English."

"No problem," the man answered. The man's name tag, Kito noticed, read: José. "Where are you going?"

"An hour south of the airport. A little village called Akumal."

"Bueno!" And they took off.

In the middle seat sat the Hollinghorsts.

Kito and Chester shared the window, taking turns falling off the seat as they kept nosing for a good view.

In the backseat, Schmitty sat beside his owner, Hillary, their Pembrook neighbor. She cooed, "Oh, look! Palm trees! I'm so looking forward to all the greenery. I can't wait to learn the names of every plant and flower. I brought a dozen identification books."

"Sea turtles!" exclaimed Mr. H. "That's what we want to see. Plus, it's part of my research for my next novel. Not only am I hoping to snorkel with them, but if we're really lucky, we'll see some of their eggs hatch too. From what I've read, it's nearing the end of their nesting season."

"Sea turtles?" Chester said. "What can possibly be so exciting about turtles and their eggs? I've seen plenty of painted turtles on our lake, and a few snapping turtles, which are definitely best to avoid."

Schmitty piped up from the back. "Remember when that boy teased a big snapper with a broom handle?"

"Criminy creature!" Chester replied. "That snapper snapped the end right off that broom. I mean, I wouldn't like somebody shoving a broom at my mouth either. But despite my American Kennel Club good breeding, there's no way I could bite off a broom handle in one chomp!"

"If sea turtles are anything like snappers," Kito said, "I think I'll steer clear. I'd like to keep my paws and nose."

Kito tried to read the billboards and road signs, but they were in another language that he couldn't make sense of at all. Must be Spanish. Maybe if he'd grown up around Spanish he'd have learned to read it, just as he had learned English. The other two dogs might be able to relax for the next seven days, but he would keep a lookout for trouble. It was his duty.

Mr. H scribbled notes on a notepad. Mrs. H sketched in her art journal. And Hillary snapped photos of every flowering bush they passed. After a time, she spoke up. "It's so nice of you two to invite me to join you on vacation. And to bring Schmitty, too. I've never been out of the country before!"

"Sharing expenses helps us out too," Mrs. H replied. "And besides, you're good company!" She looked over her shoulder and smiled.

"Our dogs will certainly have fun together. I just hope Schmitty doesn't cause any trouble."

"What kind of trouble can they possibly get into?" Mrs. H asked. "They're good dogs at home. I'm sure they'll be good dogs here in Mexico, too."

Kito, Chester, and Schmitty all exchanged glances.

Schmitty's silky black ears lifted slightly. "They have no idea the dangers we face every day at home, do they?"

"Exactly why we're going to take it easy here!" Chester said. "We don't have to keep a lookout for trouble, tangle with ill-meaning strangers, or solve a single mystery. So they're right. They don't have to worry a bit about us. What kind of trouble could we possibly get into on vacation?"

Chester's words hit Kito in the gut. His stomach tightened with a twinge of knowing. No matter how much he wished that their week away would be problem-free, his gut told him otherwise. Some kind of trouble lay ahead. He just didn't know what kind. He'd play it calm, like a dog of leisure, but on his own he'd be keeping a lookout for anything out of the ordinary.

When they turned off the highway, the van went under an archway with a turtle painted overhead. The village was as colorful as a rainbow. Restaurants with outdoor seating beckoned with red, yellow, and blue tablecloths. Small hotels and shops lined the streets. They passed an outdoor market filled with brightly colored rugs, baskets, and tables of pottery, vegetables, and fruit. And then, to Kito's surprise, he noticed two dogs wandering—unleashed. "Look!" he exclaimed.

"What?" Chester asked. "It's all a blur going by!"

"Two dogs roaming free. No leashes! Just

like in Pembrook! Maybe we won't have to be leashed while we're here."

"I wouldn't hold your breath," Schmitty said from the back. "Even towns with leash laws have a few dogs breaking the rules. Pembrook is not like most towns."

Kito didn't say another word. He'd have to find out for himself. At the first opportunity, he'd simply have to try to visit with one of the local dogs.

When they arrived at their lodging, Kito was glad to get out and stretch his legs. A roaring sound, however, made him take cover under the van. "Kito!" Mrs. H exclaimed. "What is it this time? Sometimes you're such a chicken."

He cringed. Chicken. He knew what that meant. Not at all brave. Well, he was doing his best. But what was that roaring sound?

"Dear, I think he's afraid of the ocean," said Mr. H. "He's never heard it or seen it before. Let's go dip our toes in the waves and then we'll move our luggage inside."

All on leashes, the three dogs trotted

with their owners around the side of the condo where they were going to stay. As they rounded the corner, Kito could barely believe what he was seeing. A turquoise blue expanse of water stretched on forever in front of him. Giant waves rolled, curled, and crashed in frothy bubbles against the white sand shore. So that was the deafening sound that had frightened him! He inhaled the salty, damp air and shook his coat. Maybe his gut feeling had been wrong and he'd just been a bundle of jitters. What could possibly go wrong in such a paradise?

3

A Warning

Then, with a tug at his collar, he found himself running alongside Mrs. H across hot, hot sand and right into the ocean. The water was far warmer than at home but still cooled his paws. Kito stepped out farther until the water soaked his underbelly, his sides, and his back. And then in a giant *whoosh*, a wave crashed over his head, knocked him to the sand floor of the ocean, and threatened to pull him out to the sea. He again felt a tug on his collar, took in a gulp of salty seawater, choked, and surfaced.

"That was awesome!" Schmitty called out, jumping in and out of the waves.

Chester was busy snuffling alongside Mr. H, heading down the shore. *Snuffle, snuffle, snuff, snuff.*

Mrs. H stood alongside Kito in knee-deep water. "Looks like that wave got the best of you," she said. "Let's get under the thatched hut. You need to catch your breath."

Kito hacked up a mouth full of water. His eyes burned from the salty seawater. Mrs. H was right. A little break might be just what he needed. He followed her to a thatched roof on wooden stilts. In the shade, Kito flopped down beside the lounge chair. Chester and Mr. H were becoming smaller and smaller far down the beach. Schmitty was smiling, as dogs do, running after the Frisbee that Hillary tossed for him. And here he was, already needing to get out of the sun—and waves.

And then he spotted it. Like the bald head of an old man, but much smaller. Bigger than a fist, but smaller than a football.

It was there in the water looking directly at the shore. Maybe at him!

"Did you see that, Kito?" Mrs. H said. "A sea turtle!"

Kito saw it, all right! The hairs along his spine bristled. A low growl trembled in his throat, and then he started barking. His meanest, keep-away-if-you-know-what's-good-for-you bark! *"Er-roof-roof-roof! Er-roof-roof-roof!"*

"Kito, no!" Mrs. H scolded. "People come here to relax, not to hear you bark. So no barking."

But he couldn't stop himself.

"Kito, quiet!"

But he couldn't be quiet. If that turtle's head was that big, then its body must be huge! And turtles could not only swim, he knew, but they could also walk on land. He shivered at the thought. And who knew what else the ocean held? This was a very different and strange place. He was going to have to be very, very careful! He barked and barked until the sea turtle dipped below and disappeared from sight.

Mrs. H stroked his back until he calmed down and stopped barking. If only Mrs. H knew that he was protecting not only himself. He was protecting *her*, too.

A deeply tanned man with white shorts and a T-shirt walked up to Mrs. H's lounge chair. He grabbed his straw hat, lifted it for a moment, showing a full head of curly white hair, and then put it back on again. "Mrs. Hollinghorst, perhaps?"

"Yes, that's right," she replied, keeping a firm grip on Kito's leash. He squeezed under her chair.

"*Hola!* I'm Carlos, manager of Ocean Flower condos," he said. "Welcome! I hope you feel at home in Unit Number Three."

"Yes, thank you!" Mrs. H replied. "Carlos, you speak English so well. Are you from the U.S.?"

"Born in Mexico City and went to college in Boston."

"I see," said Mrs. H. "I wish we were as fluent in Spanish! Well, we just wanted to see the ocean, and then we'll move our luggage inside."

"*Bueno*," the man said. Kito started to think *bueno* must mean "good." Then Carlos added, "I must ask that you keep your dogs under control at all times."

"On leashes, you mean?"

"Leashed or not leashed, it means making sure they do not bother other guests." He gave a nod to the small pool, where a couple was swimming with two children. "If other guests complain, then you'll have to cut your vacation short and leave early. I don't want that to happen, of course, and I know that you don't either. But I hope you understand."

Kito eased out from under the chair. Carlos looked like a nice enough man. Kito controlled himself from growling. Though he'd love to head home, he didn't want to spoil the vacation for Mr. and Mrs. H. The Hollinghorsts were good owners who worked hard to make their dogs' lives happy. It was the least he could do to not cause them to have to leave early.

"And just one more thing," Carlos added.

He pointed down the beach, which curved like a giant horseshoe from one point to the other. "Do you see those little flags on sticks?"

Kito followed Mrs. H's gaze. "Yes, I see them." Kito spotted the small red flags too, scattered halfway between the seashore and the condos and villas along the beach.

"Those are sea turtle nests," he explained. "If the dogs disturb the nests, not only will you be asked to leave, but there are some people around here who, well, would be quick to make sure that the dogs never disturb a nest again." His expression was dead serious.

"You mean—"

"I mean, don't let your dogs to disturb a single nest. The sea turtles are an endangered species and because they nest on Half Moon Bay here, they help attract many tourists. Like you. And that helps the economy here. You know, jobs for lots of locals. So, you get what I'm saying, right?"

Mrs. H's lips were pressed tightly together,

as if she was thinking hard about everything he'd just said. "Um, okay. Sure. We'll keep a close eye on our dogs." She looked down the beach. "I better let my husband and our friend know about the nests too."

"*Sí*," Carlos said with a nod. Then he smiled broadly, and the sun glinted off the silver chain around his neck. At the chain's V, a silver turtle dangled against Carlos's bronze skin. "Welcome to Mexico," he said. "I hope your stay is wonderful!"

Kito watched the man closely as he walked over to the pool guests and began visiting. There was nothing at all relaxing about this vacation, and he'd only been away from home one day. Now he had to worry over the man's warning about the turtle nests. What if Schmitty and Chester started wrestling around the nests, or digging them up for fun? Would his canine buddies disappear—the same way the sea turtle had slipped below the surface? Gone without a trace?

Trouble in Paradise

The early morning sun tinted the horizon pink. Seagulls wheeled over the beach, calling, reminding Kito of home. How was Dog Watch doing back home without three of its key members?

Stretched out at the feet of Mrs. H, Kito absorbed the cool tiles beneath him, a mosaic of blues and yellows.

"It really is paradise, isn't it?" Mrs. H mused as she sketched.

Kito wasn't so sure. Though the sun hadn't yet turned the day scorchingly hot, it was still too warm for him.

He studied Schmitty and Hillary Rothchild as they strolled down the beach past several beach rakers. Every morning, men were out, raking the beaches clean of whatever the tide had left behind. If anyone knew what went on at the beach, it would be them.

Two brown pelicans took turns swooping and diving into the ocean. They'd circle above the water, then, wings tucked, they'd dive with their long beaks pointed straight for the water. Most times they came up without a catch, but this time, the pelican lifted its neck and swallowed a fish whole.

"Mornin'," Chester said, startling Kito. Mr. H followed behind, blinking and squinting as the sun arched over the horizon. He held a mug of coffee. "Good morning, honey!" He kissed the top of Mrs. H's head, and then he bent down to scratch Kito. "And to you, too."

Kito rolled on his back to get a good belly scratching, when suddenly a voice startled him.

"*Buenos días!*" A boy about ten years old strolled up to the table.

Kito flipped back onto his paws and sat squarely, his head high and watchful. Though he didn't like strangers, this boy looked friendly. With dark hair and alert brown eyes, he smiled at Mrs. H. "*Buenos días, Señora.* My name is Juan. You like jewelry?" Dozens of necklaces and bracelets draped Juan's arm. Kito liked the one with green, amber, and brown beads best.

"They're beautiful," Mrs. H replied. "How much?"

"Two hundred *pesos* for necklaces," the boy said. "Very beautiful, *sí?*"

"Yes, that's, um, in U.S. dollars—twenty dollars, right?"

"*Sí,*" the boy replied. He slipped one of the necklaces off his arm and handed it to Mrs. H. "This one?"

Mrs. H held up the necklace of green beads to the light. "We just arrived yesterday. I don't know."

With a practiced expression of serious-ness, the boy said, "Only fifteen dollars."

Mrs. H studied the jewelry. "Mmmm."

"Best I can do," the boy said. "My father unhappy. But, for you, one hundred *pesos*."

"Ten dollars?"

"*Sí*," the boy said. "Very good price."

While Mrs. H bought necklaces and brace-lets for friends and family back home, Kito noticed that though the boy wore a clean white T-shirt and shorts, he was barefoot and walked with a limp. His left ankle was slightly swollen and red.

"What happened to your ankle?" Mr. H asked, pointing to the same spot that Kito was studying.

"Bit by a dog," the boy said. "It has no home. A stray. I walk one night." He made a biting motion with his hand.

"That's too bad," Mr. H said. "We saw a few dogs roaming the village as we drove in yesterday. Should we worry?"

The boy waved away her concerns. "No,

Señora. Most dogs. They very, very good dogs. Just sometimes."

"Hope it doesn't have rabies," Mrs. H said. "Did you see a doctor?"

The boy just nodded. Maybe "rabies" wasn't a word this boy knew in English, Kito thought. Still, that he could speak both Spanish and English was impressive! But rabies? That was another matter. A dog with rabies was dangerous. It might attack people—or visiting dogs. Kito pictured the dog. Big build. Giant teeth. A frothy mouth. Much like Spike at home.

"You see *chiquito* dog," the boy made a show with his hands of a dog smaller than Chester. *Chiquito* must mean "little"! "Stay away."

"*Sí*," replied Mr. H and Mrs. H. They thanked the boy, paid him for his wares, and waved when he headed down the beach to the next group of tourists.

"Nice boy," Mrs. H said.

Kito locked eyes with Chester. He couldn't help but tease his buddy. "Hey, Chester? Bit anybody in the ankle lately?"

27

"Just knock it off," Chester replied. "That's not funny."

Later that morning, Chester, Kito, and Schmitty sat in the bow of a large white boat. When they were farther out from shore, Mr. and Mrs. H and Hillary jumped off the boat's edge, fins first, held their masks to their faces, and slipped into the ocean.

"Snorkeling looks creepy," Schmitty said. "I don't get it. How can you go underwater with a tube and not drown?"

"You breathe through the tube, Einstein," Chester said.

"Hey, I know when you're joking. You said Einstein, who everyone knows was super smart, just to really say that I'm stupid. Didn't you?" He went nose to nose with Chester. "Just because you're a registered beagle doesn't give you the right to put down—"

"Easy, pal," Chester said, his back hair raised. "You're the one who used the word 'stupid,' not me."

"Hey, you two," Kito warned. He backed his warning up with a growl. "This is a vacation, remember? We're supposed to be taking it easy . . . having fun, right?"

Schmitty edged a few steps away from Chester and rested his head on the edge of the boat. "Well, let's just say I'd never snorkel."

"Me either," Kito agreed.

"Beefy biscuits!" said Chester. "It's not like our owners are going to rent us snorkeling equipment. I can just see it now. Dogs swimming with snorkels clamped in their teeth! Masks over their noses!"

"Yeah, we'd chew up our snorkels before we got back to the surface," Schmitty added.

An hour slipped by lazily. The sun bore down on the dogs and Kito longed to jump overboard, but he didn't dare. Fortunately, a small canvas roof covered part of the boat, and the dogs rested in the shade.

The boat driver, a man whose T-shirt was missing its sleeves, hummed to himself and waited by the idle motor while the others snorkeled.

Kito rose from the shade and decided to look for sharks. He'd watched programs on television about them. If he had any thoughts of jumping overboard to cool off, all he had to do was remind himself how many teeth sharks had in their mouths. He didn't remember exactly how many. But it was lots!

Paws to the gunwale, Kito watched. Occasionally, a bright yellow fish or striped fish swam past through the aqua blue water. And then Kito spotted it—for the second time since he'd arrived.

The head of a turtle broke the surface, took in air, and then gently dipped below again. Trembling with excitement, Kito began barking and barking. Schmitty and Chester joined in until they created a chorus of dog music.

"No!" the boat driver commanded.

Their tails dropped low and the dogs quit barking, but kept watching. And there it was again. The sea turtle! Just beyond them by a wave or two, it swam toward them, then alongside the boat, right under their noses.

"Do you see that? Do you see that?" Schmitty called.

"Criminy crackers, Schmitty! How could you miss it?"

Its greenish-brown body was almost as wide as a dog house! Kito had no idea that turtles could get that big! It must have been growing for a long, long time. It was ancient! He shivered, partly with fear, partly with amazement. Two foot-long fish swam alongside the turtle, darting in and out from beneath the turtle's shell. They must be finding food on the turtle or near it. There was so much about ocean life that Kito would never understand.

When the turtle surfaced again for air, it seemed to look straight at him. And for a moment, Kito almost wondered if the turtle was trying to communicate somehow. With a single slow blink of its eyes, the mighty turtle seemed to be asking him something. And though he didn't hear words, he was

sure he understood its plea. She said, *Please watch over the nests onshore.*

And as strange as it seemed, though dogs could only communicate through silent language with other dogs—not turtles—he heard himself promise something back to the turtle. Not in words, exactly. More from his heart. And he answered her: *While I'm here. I will. I promise.*

Then she swam under the boat and away. Kito looked and looked for her. But she was gone. And he was left with a strong urge to get back to the beach at Half Moon Bay and make sure the nests were okay.

5

A Promise Made

Kito kept his encounter with the sea turtle to himself. He didn't want Chester and Schmitty to think he'd lost his brains. Communicating with sea turtles wasn't something they'd probably want to hear about. But in his heart, Kito knew what he knew. He'd made a promise to protect the nests, at least for the duration of his time on Half Moon Bay.

The next morning, after another round of Hearty Hound (the Hollinghorsts had brought dog food), the dogs hiked the beach with their owners and the condo manager.

Like a tour guide, Carlos led them all down the beach. In leather sandals, red swim trunks, and an unbuttoned shirt, he paused beside small mounds of sand sporting red flags. "This nest," he said, "was the first to be found. So it's number one." He walked a few more paces. "And this one, number eight, was found later." He pointed up and down the beach. "All in all, we've marked eighty-two nests on this bay alone, and sixty of those nests have already hatched. That leaves twenty-two to go. Every day could bring new babies. That's why we have teams of observers—people who keep an eye on which nests are hatching and when."

Mrs. H squatted beside nest number eight. "So right now there are little turtles in their shells just waiting to hatch and crawl out?"

"*Sí, Señora.* And it's when they hatch that they are the most vulnerable. It's a dangerous time. So we try to help them survive."

Mr. H busily wrote on a notepad. "What kind of dangers exactly?"

Kito was all ears. If he was going to keep his promise, then he needed to know what kind of risks these nests—and their hatchlings—faced.

"Birds of prey, for one. Seagulls and pelicans are quick to make a snack of them. Their shells are soft when they first hatch and offer little protection."

"But the mothers," Mrs. H began. "Don't they come back from the sea and guide their babies to the water when they hatch?"

"*No, Señora.* That would be great, but it's not the way it works. Once the eggs are laid, the mother leaves and the babies are on their own to hatch, make the trek to the water, and swim out there—beyond the coral reef."

Kito pictured pelicans diving from the air into the water to catch their prey. A baby sea turtle would be an easy snack!

"What other kind of dangers?" Mr. H pressed. He kept taking notes.

"People who don't know better. Sometimes tourists. Anyone who thinks it's fun to dig up turtle nests."

"Criminy," Chester said as he snuffled around the nest. "That's not very nice, is it, Kito?"

"Got that right."

Carlos continued talking with the Hollinghorsts and gave a nod to Kito and Chester. "Dogs are another risk. Some like to dig up the nests. Hungry dogs will eat the eggs. Your dog there—he's sniffing pretty hard. You'll keep an eye on him, *sí*?"

"Oh, yes!" Mrs. H said. She pulled a leash out of the pocket of her floral sundress. "If they show any signs of misbehaving, they'll be on leashes. But really, they're good dogs."

"The best," agreed Mr. H.

Kito wondered if Chester could resist digging if he caught the scent of something stirring below. He'd seen his buddy come across the scent of a rabbit before, and there was no stopping his beagle buddy then. "Hey, Chester," he said. "You wouldn't do anything stupid, would you, like dig up one of these nests, would you?"

Snuffle, snuff, snuff. "Who, me?" Chester kept circling the nest, his black button nose sugared with sand. "Never smelled anything quite like this before! It's, well . . ." *Snuffle, snuff, snuff, snuff.* "It's extremely interesting, that's what!"

"Hey, pal. Just don't get carried away. Back off or we'll end up being leashed the rest of our time here."

"I know!"

Kito hoped to distract Chester from getting too serious about sniffing. "Let's play tag!" Front feet in the air, he came down in the sand beside Chester and made him jump.

"Gotcha!" Kito cried, threatening to nip at Chester's hind legs until Chester spun around, ran off, and turned several tight circles. Then they took turns chasing each other up and down the beach.

Stopping to catch his breath, Kito looked back over his shoulder at the Hollinghorsts. They had moved down the beach and were now standing beside a different nest. They were shaking their heads. And their new friend, Carlos, was pressing his palm to his forehead. Mr. H stooped to look closer at the nest, which was now a deep hole. Something was definitely wrong!

Kicking up sand, he left Chester behind and ran over to take a look.

Panting in the heat, he peered down into the damp base of the hole. The mysterious smells of sea life floated up. At the nest's base, where he expected to see whole eggs, was a scattering of broken and smashed eggshells. His heart lifted. That must mean the turtles had hatched and crawled to the ocean.

"This is bad," Carlos said.

Kito looked up. Carlos squared his hands to his hips. "Very bad. This nest was not reported online as having hatched. I just checked this morning. We have night teams and morning teams that count every nest and mark its activity. They would have seen this and reported it. No, this must have happened rather recently. Someone came in, did the damage, and left in a hurry."

"But maybe the turtles hatched and made it to the sea?" Mrs. H asked hopefully.

Carlos shook his head. "When they do, they leave behind cracked shells, not broken to pieces like this." He shook his head. "This is very, very sad. Something—or someone—raided this nest. And from the looks of it, they either stole the baby turtles or ate them."

Kito thought of the giant sea turtle and the way she had looked at him. There was not a more gentle creature in the world, he realized. Everything about her from her eyes to the way she dipped softly to the bottom to feed on the ocean floor, to the way she bobbed up for a breath of air . . . He could never quite describe to anybody what he felt, but the sea turtle seemed the most peaceful and wise being he'd ever encountered. And now its babies were destroyed? He'd promised to watch over the nests, and already, on his watch, a whole nest had been ruined. His tail drooped low.

"No wonder they're on the endangered

species list," Mr. H said. Barefooted, he squatted beside the empty nest and Kito. Absently, he scratched Kito between the ears. "Well, our dogs have been with us every moment since we've arrived," he said, "so I can assure you they aren't to blame for this upset."

"I'm glad to hear that," Carlos said, looking up and down the beach. "Because when I catch whoever destroyed this nest—" His unfinished thought hung on the sea breeze. "This makes me so angry."

Kito wasn't going to tell about his almost magical encounter with the sea turtle, but he was going to get Schmitty and Chester together for a meeting. They may only be a team of three, and they surely were *not* in Pembrook, but that didn't matter. It was time for Dog Watch to take action!

6

Watch out, *Amigos!*

At the earliest opportunity, which proved to be right before dinner, Kito gathered Chester and Schmitty in the living room. They weren't allowed in the condo to lie around on the two couches, so instead they sprawled on the woven rug by the patio door—with a great view of the ocean. Kito loved the shades of blue and turquoise, the ever-changing size of waves, the way they curled like whipped cream. But he had to turn away and set all that beauty aside.

"Dog Watch," he began. "Called to order."

"Huh?" Chester said, cocking his head. "Give me a break. We're on vacation, remember? It's *siesta* time!"

"That's right," Schmitty added. "We don't need to pretend to have a mission. We can take a break, Kito. It's okay to relax once in a while. I'm sure Tundra and the others are on duty back home. We don't need to be."

"I'm serious," Kito pressed on. His neck arced as he sat on his haunches. Better to tower over them a little to get their attention. "I'm not drumming up some wild ideas. Half Moon Bay is the nesting ground to hundreds of sea turtles. And one of those nests was destroyed last night—before its babies were able to hatch."

Chester licked at his paws. "So, what does that have to do with us? We don't live here."

"Well, remember the oath we took?"

Chester and Schmitty repeated the oath halfheartedly. *"Day or night, Pembrook dogs unite."*

"Well, I don't think our oath limits us to only Pembrook. I mean, this is a village, too.

We're here. There's a crisis. And maybe, just maybe, we can help solve it. It's a chance to do something good."

"So who would bother to hurt baby sea turtles?" Schmitty asked, sitting up.

Chester rose slowly to his legs, stretched his head toward his paws, then stood tall. "Criminy, this one stretches my imagination. I think we're completely out of our element, Kito. What do we know about ocean life and turtle nests?"

Kito explained what he'd heard from Carlos—how the sea turtles were an endangered species, how they laid their eggs in the sand, and how people or animals or birds could threaten the nests and the whole future of sea turtles. He also explained how vulnerable the baby turtles were as they made the trek from their nest in the sand to the sea.

"You really care about these little turtles, don't you?" Schmitty asked.

"Oh," Kito said with a shrug. He didn't want to let on just how much the turtles had touched his heart. After all, he was of chow chow breeding, and everyone expected him to be a little gruff with everyone except family and the closest of friends. "Yeah, I guess I care. A little."

Together they discussed what to do, and finally agreed to be watchful, to do what they could if they came across anyone causing trouble. And in the meantime, Kito agreed they could still take plenty of naps—as long as they took turns keeping watch. After all, they *were* on vacation.

"Just smell these fish!" Hillary said, tending the grill. From aluminum foil packages on the grill came a delicious aroma of onions, peppers, and sizzling fish. When dinner was served, Kito sat near Mrs. H, his mouth watering. He waited patiently, and during dishes she offered each dog a small taste. "This is grouper," she said. "And I double-checked for bones."

The dogs smacked their lips, hoping for more. The next course was Hearty Hound.

Life didn't get much better than that.

Belly full, Kito wandered beyond the pool to the expanse of sand that stretched a stone's throw to the water. He dropped down, rested his head on his paws, and watched the sky darken to shades of gray as the sun dipped behind him.

It had been a long day and he was tired, but glad for the cooler evening temperatures. Suddenly, a *scritch-scratching* stirred him. Someone was trying to sneak around on the beach.

Ears perked, he sat up on his haunches, listening to the full extent of his dog abilities.

Scritch-scritch-scratch.

Maybe someone was bothering the turtle nests! He growled, but the noise continued. "Chester! Schmitty!" he called out. He barked for extra emphasis. They were in the condo, sleeping, just beyond the screen door. Soon, they stirred, and whined to be let out.

Mrs. H let them outside. "Don't go too far, boys. It's getting late."

"Think they should be leashed?" Hillary asked.

"They've been good. They'll be right back."

Chester and Schmitty trotted up to Kito's side and stood together in the settling darkness. "What's up?" Chester asked.

"Listen." Kito held still and waited. For a few moments it was silent, and then—*scritch, scratch, scratch*. "Hear it?"

Schmitty trotted straight toward the sound, but Kito and Chester held back, waiting for a report.

"Hey," Schmitty called back. He nosed around a few small plants. "You guys have gotta see this!"

Cautiously, Kito stepped closer. His eyes adjusted to the dark. And then he saw it: a paw slinking out from behind its hiding place. His back hairs shot up. The paw moved. A dog! Only, there was nothing else attached to the paw. It was a . . . He didn't know what to make of it. It crawled across the sand. And then, from beneath the protection of several plants, there were more. Two, three, four, five, six! Not paws at all, but big shells in motion!

"Criminy cripes!" Chester cried out, stepping backward, then inching forward again. "What are they?"

"Don't you know?" Schmitty said, his ears perked up with enthusiasm. "Hermit crabs! But I didn't know they lived here."

Chester sniffed, nose to the ground. He went right up to a shell the size of a tennis ball. "Ouch!"

He jumped back and the crab dangled from Chester's nose. "Get it off me!" he yelped. "Help! Help! Get it off!"

Schmitty grabbed the shell in his teeth, gave a quick pull, and the crab let go. Then he set the shell gently on the ground. "There you go, little guy."

Kito watched the hermit crab. For a moment it didn't move, and he didn't see any claws at all. Then the creature lifted itself, stretched out its little crab legs, and continued on its path to the sea.

"Oh, my beautiful beagle nose," Chester whined, batting at his black nose with his paw. "What if this affects my super abilities to sniff out trouble? Then what will you do without me? This is a near tragedy. Good gravy and biscuits!"

"Chester," Schmitty said. "It didn't mean to hurt you. It was just trying to protect itself. You got too close, that's all."

"Is my nose bleeding? I hate the sight of blood. Is it?!"

Kito studied it and sniffed. "It's not. You're gonna live." He turned to Schmitty. "How do you know about hermit crabs?"

"Hillary used to have one as a pet, that's

how. As they grow they find a bigger shell. That's why they come in all sizes." He motioned to the troop of hermit crabs making their way to the shore. "Let's follow them."

"Okay," Chester said, "but at a distance!"

Slowly the crabs walked with their shell homes toward the water. They stopped just at the crest of sand before it dropped below to the surf. "Wonder why they're stopping here?" Kito mused.

Schmitty sat down, clearly at ease around these creatures. "Must be a good place to find food that washes up."

Kito sat down too. The hermit crabs were gathering in greater numbers—their own little beach party. Overhead, stars glittered on a velvety black blanket. The night was perfect, and filled with new discoveries. He wondered if any sea turtles were stirring in their shells, getting ready to make the trek from their nests to the sea. Oh, he'd love to be there to see them hatch.

Suddenly, growling shattered the moment.

And it came from only a few yards away from them on the beach.

"Amigos!" warned a dog with a gravelly voice. "Get off my beach or you're going to find yourself chewed to pieces!" The strange dog started barking, then dropped its voice back to a menacingly low growl. "I tell you. I am your worst nightmare. Do not mess with me!"

Tail between his legs, Chester turned and ran back to the condo.

Kito and Schmitty stood their ground.

The darkness was so complete that, even at a few yards off, Kito could not see the dog. But he could hear its labored breathing.

"Well, *amigos*. If you will not run away," the dog said, inching closer, his voice less menacing, "maybe we will have to be friends."

A thousand shivers ran down Kito's back. Now he could see the dog, at least clearly enough to note it was a shadowy dog. Small and gray, with a scruffy coat. And it exactly

matched the description of the dog that had bit that boy's ankle. The boy who sold jewelry. The dog that might have rabies. And any animal with rabies might act friendly, but it was deadly dangerous with the hidden plan of biting and passing on its disease! A dog with rabies was a crazy dog.

"Run!" Kito cried out. "Rabies! Run!"

He and Schmitty bolted for the condo, veered under the thatched hut, nearly slipped in the pool, made it to the screen door, and yipped at full volume!

"Let us in!"

7

A Dog Named Chico

How can a dog possibly sleep well after a near-death encounter with a rabid animal? Kito couldn't. He tossed and turned all night on the woven rug. But at least they'd outrun the dog on the beach who had come out of the shadows to attack them. They'd escaped, but barely.

When Mr. and Mrs. H woke up, they poured themselves cups of coffee and sat on the patio. The sun painted the horizon in pinks and golds. Kito drew a deep breath, let the tension ease off his paws, and settled at his owners' feet beneath the table.

He fell into a good sleep, and this time dreamed of swimming underwater. Underwater! What a thrill to dive in, eyes open, and see everything below. Brightly colored fish swam past him, and a sea turtle swam alongside him. He knew it was the same turtle he'd watched from the boat the other day. She reminded him again that the turtles needed his help. *"Can you help us?"* she asked, in a voice both soft and strong. He wanted to answer, but before he could, he realized that he was underwater and that dogs don't swim underwater and he gulped for air but instead breathed in salty seawater. Then the tide began pulling him deeper, out to sea. He cried for help and thrashed for the surface. . . . "Kito, honey," Mrs. H said, stroking his fur. "You're crying and twitching. Must be having a bad dream."

He stood up, shook out his coat, and tried to shake the dream from his head. He never wanted a drowning dream again. But the part about the turtle—he liked that part.

"*Buenos días!*" said Carlos. The condo manager stepped around the corner of the building to greet the Hollinghorsts. He tipped his hat toward Mrs. H, and Kito noted that Carlos was not dressed for the beach. From head to toe he sparkled with a red tie, white shirt, linen trousers, and polished shoes. He definitely wasn't heading out to collect seashells.

"Before I go to Cancún for a meeting," he said, "I must discuss your dogs."

"Oh, I'm sorry," Mr. H said. "It's about their noise last night?"

"I'm afraid so," Carlos said. He combed his fingers through his hair. "A few complaints from other guests. They must be kept quiet, *sí*?"

"Yes, yes," Mr. H replied. "Something scared them on the beach last night and they yipped and complained to be let in right away. I wonder what it was."

Carlos looked off to sea. "Some say this region is haunted by ships that went down on coral reefs long ago."

Kito trembled at the thought. Haunted? Was that dog a ghost dog?

"Sometimes turtles climb onto the beach. Or perhaps your dogs were stung by the tentacles of a jellyfish that floated up."

"Hmmm. Maybe that's it. Our beagle's nose seemed a little swollen."

"Well, that might explain it," Carlos said. "But no matter the cause, we cannot have them making too much noise. I would hate to have to ask you to leave."

Mrs. H looked as if she might cry. "I hope not."

Kito vowed to keep himself under control, and to remind Chester and Schmitty to do the same. He'd feel awful if his owners and Hillary Rothchild had to cut their vacation short because of them.

After Carlos left, Mr. and Mrs. H read books as the sun climbed higher. Kito stayed in the shade of the table, but kept a watchful eye on the beach. He wanted to explore the whole beach to see if any nests had been disturbed, but for the moment, it seemed prudent to stay put and let the Hollinghorsts know that he wasn't causing a speck of trouble.

"You like jewelry?" came a voice. He had slipped up to the table so quietly that Kito hadn't noticed him. It was Juan, the same boy who had come by earlier.

Hillary stepped out of the condo.

"Hey, what's shakin'?" Chester asked, following behind.

Schmitty joined them too. "Any turtle troubles?"

"Yes!" Hillary said to Carlos. "I would love to see what you have. I missed you the other day." She sat down at a free chair, and Juan showed her his bracelets and necklaces.

And that's when Kito noticed the dog, lurking at the edge of the pool. It was the same gray dust mop dog from last night. He couldn't help himself. He started barking out a warning. "Don't take another step closer!" he warned.

"Hey! Down there!" someone called from the balcony above. "Keep your dogs quiet.

We're trying to sleep up here!"

Kito felt a sharp yank on his collar. Mr. H pulled him to his side and said in a no-nonsense-better-listen-up voice, "Kito, sit!"

He sat and shut his mouth. He had to control himself—or else. But what if that dog had rabies? Wouldn't it be better to warn everyone and to keep them safe?

Juan squatted on the ground. "Chico!" he called in a friendly voice. He held out his hand to the dog.

"What's he doing?" Chester asked, sniffing the air and hopping up on Mrs. H's lap. "That dog's a killer. Our worst nightmare, remember?"

Schmitty sat squarely beside Hillary as she looked through the jewelry spread across the table. He was clearly protecting her.

Chico, the little scruffy gray dog, walked closer to Juan.

"Is this the one that bit you?" Mrs. H asked, a hint of worry in her voice.

"*Sí, Señora*," Juan said. "But now—we friends."

Chico slunk down, nearly pressing his belly to the ground, then crawled humbly to the boy. When he reached Juan's outstretched hand, Kito nearly jumped out of his skin. He was certain it was all an act and that this rabid dog was going to bite—but it didn't. Instead, it rolled onto its back, let Juan scratch its belly, and licked at Juan's hand. That wasn't the behavior of a mean dog or a rabid dog. It could only mean one thing. The dog was friendly. At least with Juan.

"See? He good. *Bueno!*" Juan looked from the Hollinghorsts and Hillary and back to Chico. "Now my dog."

"Do you think he bit you because he was scared of you?" Mrs. H asked.

"*Sí, sí.* He scared I—" Carlos pretended to pick up something and hit at the air.

"Oh, hit him," Hillary said, her eyes full of understanding. "He had been hit before, and so he was scared of you?"

"*Sí, Señora!*" Juan's eyes lit up. "Now all change. He my dog." He patted Chico's thin sides. "Now with my home."

"So he lives with you now?" Mrs. H asked.

"*Sí.* Before," Juan said, shaking his head sadly and pointing to the beach, "only beach dog."

Kito looked at this little dog and wondered why he had been so afraid of it last night. It wasn't scary at all.

"So," he said to Chico, "you were a beach dog? How did you get food?"

"From people," Chico replied. "In the village, at one shop, they put out bowls of food. Just for hungry dogs with no homes."

"But now you have a home?"

"Ah, *sí, amigo*!" He licked Juan's hand again.

"But, wait," Chester said. "I don't get it. You're speaking two languages. How come you speak English if you're a beach dog?"

"My friends," Chico said sadly, "I wasn't always a beach dog. Years ago, like you, I came here on vacation with my owners. But I got lost . . . in the jungle. They returned to California without me. Make sure you don't wander too far, *amigos*."

Kito, Chester, and Schmitty inched closer together.

"But now I have a question for you," Chico announced. "Are you the ones who destroyed a turtle nest the other morning?"

"No, why would we do that?"

"Somebody has been on this beach," Chico said. "Somebody has been doing bad things," the dog continued. "And this most recent destruction happened after you arrived."

"Not us," Kito said. "We don't want to cause any trouble, especially with turtle nests. It wasn't us."

"You're sure? You're telling the truth?" Chico asked. He looked to Chester and Schmitty as if reading their souls for dark spots of dishonesty. Maybe living on the beach made a dog less trustful, Kito thought.

"Criminy biscuits!" Chester piped up. "We're Dog Watch members. Of course we tell the truth. And Kito's more honest than any dog you'll ever meet in your life."

"I second that," Schmitty said.

"Well, then, maybe I can trust you. Maybe," the dog said with a mixture of hesitancy and hope. "Maybe we can work together. But first, what is this thing you call 'Dog Watch'?"

8

Dog Watch International

Never in Kito's wildest dog dreams did he imagine that Dog Watch could work somewhere else in the world. But that morning, while Juan and the Hollinghorsts and Hillary Rothchild visited about jewelry and life in Mexico, the dogs trotted to the village center.

Chico talked the whole way there. He explained to Kito, Chester, and Schmitty that it worked very much the same way in Akumal. Dogs could roam free as long as they had tags on their collars. The village made sure beach dogs wore tags, even if they didn't have owners. Out of kindness, villagers set out bowls of dog food every day.

They passed shops, restaurants, and small hotels. Chico called out in Spanish to a few dogs, and they replied in the same language.

Outside a pottery shop, something sitting on a wooden chair startled Kito. He widened his stance, bracing himself for trouble. But the thing didn't move. It was a skeleton! Fur on edge, Kito slowly stepped closer. He sniffed at the bony legs and arms and growled.

Schmitty and Chester circled, sniffed, and began barking at the motionless figure of death.

"*Amigos,*" Chico said. "Not to worry. There are lots of skeletons here like this one. Sometimes in paintings, carvings, and sometimes like this here. Just taking a rest!" He laughed at his joke.

Kito didn't find anything about a human skeleton funny. It was creepy. And, even creepier, it wore a purple hat with a flower and jewelry around its bony neck. He backed away, willing the hairs along his spine to calm down.

"A reminder, of sorts," Chico explained, "that no amount of money can keep a person young forever. Death and life are intertwined, you see." Then, as if to switch the subject, Chico stepped to the next shop with a thatched roof. "Come. Look here, *amigos*!" Outside the brightly painted green, yellow, and blue door, six large dog food bowls lined the shop's stucco wall.

"*Hola!*" a woman sang out. She wedged

open the door to her clothing shop and set a stool outside with a bucket labeled FEED THE BEACH DOGS. DONATE HERE. It was in English, which Kito was able to read. Other words around the village that he couldn't decipher he figured were Spanish words. It was strange. He could perfectly understand Chico, but he couldn't read Spanish. At least he could read one language. He liked that villagers were asking tourists to help out by donating.

An English-speaking family walked over from the nearby outdoor restaurant. The man, woman, and three boys all wore matching red T-shirts that read TURTLE BAKERY AND CAFÉ. They must be worried about sticking together, Kito thought. He shuddered at the thought of getting lost and missing the flight home with the Hollinghorsts.

"Mommy! Mommy! Mommy!" exclaimed the smallest boy. "Puppies!" The child toddled over toward the dogs.

"Let's go!" Chico called out, spinning away from the approaching child. He darted in the direction of the Akumal Dive Shop. "Follow me! *Rápido! Rápido!*"

The dogs gave chase, leaving the boy calling out to them. "Come back!"

They paused outside a bustling shop filled with masks and snorkels, flippers, swimsuits, and sunscreen. Kito caught his breath. "Why the rush? What was wrong back there?"

"Hombre," Chico said, scratching furiously at his left ear with his hind foot. "Some kids are good, but some kids are mean. I've had my ears pulled and I've been forced to ride in a backpack for a whole afternoon. Now I stay clear."

Diving instructors and students milled about outside the shop. Some wore heavy oxygen tanks strapped to their backs. Others were busy zipping themselves into black diving outfits. Kito thought of his underwater dream and shuddered. He'd never want to breathe through some flimsy equipment underwater. Dogs were meant to live on land.

"This Dog Watch you told me about," Chico said. "I like the idea of dogs working together." He glanced out at Akumal Bay. "This is the bay where everyone tries to swim with the turtles," Chico said. "But it's Half Moon Bay where the turtles lay their eggs.'"

"You said you have something in the village to show us," Schmitty said. "Something that might give us an idea who might be digging up the nests."

"*Sí*. Just around the corner." He led them under the shade of an archway to a brick building. "This is the Eco Center." The doors were wide open, and Chico led them inside. Display after display showed ocean life—a whole painting of brightly colored fish, two different kinds of sea turtles, octopus, stingray, man-of-war, squid, crabs, and more. Another display was all about sea coral and its various shapes and patterns. Kito had no idea there were so many different kinds: brain coral, star coral, spiral coral, stag coral. . . . Another display showed how the tides went in and out every day. No wonder the shoreline changed so much from morning until night!

And quietly standing behind a case of sea turtle eggs stood a woman with thick glasses and a magnifying glass. Strands of gray hair fell out from her lavender bandanna as she studied the display of a sea turtle nest—a dozen or so eggs clustered in the sand. "We need more eggs," she said, her voice like a frog's with a bad cold.

The dogs stood on the opposite side of the case and, in unison, sat down and looked up at the case and the woman. Her teeth were slightly crooked, and she frowned at the dogs. "You're not here to cause trouble, I hope."

The dogs wagged their tails.

"I see. You want treats."

Chico said to the other dogs, "You guys are catching on fast."

The woman, whose name tag stated DR. BRITA, reached into a nearby cupboard, pulled out dog biscuits, and tossed one to each of the dogs. "There you go," she croaked. "Now run along."

Kito crunched gratefully on the treat. But he didn't want to run along. He wanted to know everything this woman knew about sea turtle nests.

"You," she said, pointing at him with her dimpled chin. "You seem way too interested in this display of eggs. I hope you're not causing trouble out there. These eggs are like gold. In each one lies the life of a sea turtle. And if their eggs should suddenly vanish or get wiped out, then the sea turtles themselves would eventually die out. We can't let that happen. I can't let that happen."

Kito listened closely.

"My volunteers will be checking in soon," she said. "Now you dogs run along. Shoo!" She waved them away, and Kito tagged along after the other dogs.

Just outside the Eco Center, the dogs met a group of college-age students. Two young women and a young man approached, all wearing shorts, flip-flops, and tank tops. "I can't believe I missed a hatching last night," the boy said, his voice whiny and his skin much too pink from the sun. Beneath his fluff of red hair his nose was lathered thick with white sunscreen. "We combed the beaches, marking down any changes, and somehow, a whole nest hatched without my seeing it! I mean, I came all the way from Iowa to see turtles hatch and I keep missing them."

"Hey, Jenks, you're getting credit for your work," said the girl with the black ponytail. "So be happy. Besides, after you check in with Dr. Brita, you can go back to bed—or lie in the sun all afternoon until we're back on night shift duty."

Then they disappeared inside. With the doors wedged wide open, the dogs lingered, listening.

Kito turned to Chico and the other two dogs. "So teams of people patrol the beaches . . ."

"Night—and daytime, too," Chico said. "Maybe you'd call it People Watch, sí?"

Kito tried to picture how a nest could get damaged if so many people were patrolling the beaches for the sea turtles' safety. "I don't get it. Why would anyone want to hurt a nest?"

Chico let out a huff. "Kito, you have lived a sheltered life, haven't you?"

Kito thought of his village of Pembrook and all the problems he'd helped solve. "No, not exactly sheltered. I've seen my share of bad things."

"Well, one thing about being a beach dog—being homeless—is you see some of the best and the worst in people . . . and dogs. There are people who seem to have been born mean. It's that type of person who would hurt a nest, just because it might seem like fun."

At that thought, Kito had a strong urge to grip his teeth around the leg of anyone who could be so heartless. "So who are our possible culprits?" he asked.

Schmitty volunteered first. "Dr. Brita. That woman back there. She's a scientist of some sort, and scientists are often needing specimens to study. Why couldn't it be her?"

"Because she gave us biscuits, stupid," Chester said, with a confident toss of his head.

"That does it, moron," Schmitty rifled back. He tackled Chester by nipping at his front legs until Chester flopped on his back in surrender.

"Say you're sorry," Schmitty demanded. "Say it."

"Oh, criminy. Sorry."

"That wasn't really heartfelt, but it was an apology." Schmitty stepped back and let Chester rise to his legs.

"Guys," Kito said. "Can you just get along? We have work to do."

"Seems more like we're getting nowhere," Chester complained. "It's getting hot. I'm ready to head back, take a dip in the ocean, then nap somewhere shady."

Just then, angry voices floated from within the Eco Center. "There are only ten nests left to hatch!" Dr. Brita shouted. "For all I know, they could hatch out by tomorrow. And where would that leave us?"

"But I didn't sign up to take eggs from nests," one of the college girls complained.

The dogs looked at one another, ears perked, listening intently.

"That might be," Dr. Brita said, "but a scientific program needs funding, and to have funding we need proper displays of what we're studying. And right now, what we have to work with is pathetic. If all goes as planned, by next year our center will be four times as large, with whole rooms of sand and preserved nests for tourists to see—not just during the nesting season, but all year long!"

"But does that mean the eggs we take would never hatch?" one of the girls asked. "Is that even legal?"

"Miss Kaitlyn," Dr. Brita said. "Of course it's legal—as long as I have a permit, which I do. But it's a small price to pay for raising public awareness, to increase scientific understanding, and to help the overall economy of this village. Now isn't that so?"

"Oh, I don't know . . ." Kaitlyn sounded sad and uncertain.

Jenks stepped forward. "But, Dr. Brita, I think—"

"No more 'but Dr. Brita's,'" she said, cutting him off. "To get proper funding, we need proper displays. Tonight. Bring me the gold. It's your last chance. Don't blow it or I'll see that you're on the next plane back to the States. Now go. Get some rest and we'll convene back here this afternoon."

"Hear that?" Chico said, motioning the dogs closer into a huddle outside. "Something about tonight. So, Dog Watch, what are we going to do about it?"

"Meet up on the beach when it gets dark," Schmitty said.

"Sneak out and stay out until we catch the nest robbers," Chester said, his tail wagging.

"Stick together," Kito chimed in as the students walked out of the Eco Center. "No matter what."

9

Beach Bungle

Rather than take the road back from the village, the dogs followed the shoreline. The sun was high in the sky, and Schmitty, with his glistening black fur, complained the loudest. "I'm going to be a deep-fried Labrador retriever if I don't find some shade soon!"

Kito, too, needed to find a place to cool off.

"I know," Chester said, speeding up as they drew near the condo. "A dash into the ocean, and then a nap."

"*Bueno!*" Chico agreed. "Now you know why we like *siestas*."

The sand burned Kito's paws, and though he still feared the power of the ocean, he caught up to Chester and together they dashed into the water. The waves lapped at his underbelly. He let a gentle wave wash over his back, cooling him instantly. "Ahhhh. So much better."

Schmitty pounced after a clear plastic bottle that washed up with a wave. "Got it!" Schmitty called, racing in and out of the waves. But when a roller spun him on his back and carried the bottle onto the shore, Chester picked it up next.

"Finders keepers!" he shouted, twisting and turning, bottle proudly in his teeth. He stumbled, dropped the bottle, and Chico bulleted in next to claim the prize.

"*Amigos!* Catch me if you can!"

Kito was all set to give chase, especially now that his coat was soaking wet and he felt much cooler, and then movement nearby on the beach stopped him. He turned his head.

And that's when Kito saw them. A line of tiny turtles were crawling from a rough hole on the beach, each one heading in the direction of the water. Sea turtle babies! At first glance he counted eight or nine, but the closer he looked, there had to be at least twelve. "Dogs! Look!"

The other dogs stopped, looked in the direction Kito pointed his nose, and began yipping and barking.

"No! Don't disturb them," Kito called out, just as Schmitty and Chester ran to the turtles, dropped to their bellies and, tails up and wagging, yapped with excitement.

"Don't eat them!" Kito yelled, dashing in to join them. Belly to the sand, he rested right across from Chester. The turtles were no bigger than his own paws. A greenish-brown turtle with a crisscross pattern on its back crawled across the hot sand, between the dogs' noses, and headed toward the sea.

A shiver traveled from Kito's ears to his tail. "This is amazing!" he whispered. "I really had hoped to see one of these nests hatch like this. Think of it! They know which direction to go as soon as they leave the nest. They just head right to the safety of the sea."

The turtles were focused, paddling through the sand with their tiny webbed feet as their little turtle tails trailed back and forth behind them. In their wake, each turtle left tiny squiggly markings.

"One moment they're inside shells in the sand," Schmitty whispered. "The next, they're crawling out into daylight."

"I've always missed the hatchings," Chico said. "I witnessed just one when I was a puppy. It's almost like magic, isn't it?"

"Yes, magical," Kito agreed. He suddenly felt that he was actually helping fulfill his vow to keep the nests safe. He'd make sure every single turtle from this nest made it safely into the water. If anyone tried to hurt, eat, or steal one of the turtles, he'd chase them away.

Another turtle passed in front of his nose, following directly behind the previous turtle.

Ruining everything, shouts and footsteps suddenly drew closer. "Sea turtles! They're hatching!"

Kito glanced up to see a growing group of beach walkers. People. *Strangers*. As long as they were just coming to observe, that was fine. But he hoped that everyone would leave the turtles alone to make their important trek.

"Shoo!" someone shouted. "Dogs, get away from them!"

"They're trying to eat them!" yelled another.

"Help! Somebody get these dogs out of here!"

"They must be after the turtles!"

If he could only explain, Kito would tell the people that they meant no harm. Only help. But in a swirl of motion, before he knew what had exactly happened, two beach rakers showed up, grabbed the dogs by their collars—one in each hand—and hauled them away from the shore.

"They don't understand!" Kito exclaimed, trying to resist with his back feet in the sand. "We weren't going to hurt them!"

"Amigo," Chico said, being dragged along by the same beach raker, "you know that I know that, but they don't know that. I'm afraid we were in the wrong place at the wrong time, *hombre.*"

"Barkin' beef biscuits!" Chester whined. "Now what's going to happen to us?"

Schmitty yelped. "Hey, do you have to hold my collar so tight? Give me a break!"

The beach rakers paused with the dogs by a storage shed, tied a length of twine to each of their collars, and then walked them toward the condo. One knocked on the glass door, but there was no answer. The Hollinghorsts and Hillary must have been on a walk farther down the beach. Kito wanted to tell the men to just leave them in the shade. They'd be fine. Their owners would return soon.

The men spoke in Spanish, and Kito couldn't understand their speech. They seemed to come to some decision, because in a few moments, they loaded the dogs in the condominium's van—the one that shuttled tourists back and forth from the airport— and drove away.

"Think they're shipping us back home?" Schmitty asked.

"No, they can't do that without airline tickets," Kito replied.

"They wouldn't be shipping me anywhere," Chico said. "I could only be so lucky. I would love to find my owners in California. Or land somewhere exotic. Somewhere where there's snow!"

"Jumping Jack terriers!" Chester moaned.

"They're going to destroy us! Have us put to sleep!"

At that, all the dogs remained silent. Chester had put into words every dog's worst fear.

The dogs flattened themselves to the floor of the van. With each bump in the road, each pothole and winding corner, Kito's stomach ached. How could they have been so terribly misunderstood? And for watching and protecting the sea turtles, they were being hauled away—maybe to face the end of their lives? This was a great, serious, and terrible injustice!

10

Jailed

"I've seen the inside of this cell more times than I can count," Chico lamented. "But that was when I had no owner. Now I have Juan! I shouldn't be in here, especially when I was doing nothing wrong."

The room was cement from floor to walls to ceiling, and in the corner lay a toothless dog named Julio. "He comes here to sleep," Chico explained. "The pound has the coolest floor in the whole village."

Kito had to agree. On the backside of the small police station was the pound. When the two beach rakers unloaded the dogs, Kito had been certain it was to face a firing squad or the lethal injection that meant being "put to sleep." So getting herded into a shady, cool cement cell seemed like a good alternative. Instead of being depressed, he was happy to be alive!

But the hours dragged by slowly.

"What if our owners never find us?" Schmitty asked. "I mean, the beach rakers spoke only Spanish. Our owners speak only English. And Carlos, the manager, he's away for a meeting—otherwise he might have been around to interpret."

"What if we spend the rest of our lives in this cell?" Chester added. He rested his floppy beagle ears and nose upon his paws. "To have been bred for greatness, to have come from royal English breeding, only to sink to this level. If my AKC registered Beagle parents could see this now, it would break their hearts."

"Does he always go on about his breeding?" Chico asked.

"Yup," Schmitty and Kito said in unison.

"This cell might help him get over it, *sí*?"

"Royal rottweilers!" Chester said, then humphed. Then he closed his eyes firmly and said, "I don't expect any of you to understand my personal pain."

"Give me a break," Schmitty said. "The pain I'm feeling is hunger. It must be time for dinner soon."

Chico stretched up to the base of the iron-barred window. "Sun's dropping lower. My stomach's growling, too."

Kito knew he had to try to rally some team spirit, but he felt so discouraged that it wasn't easy. He tried to think. What would Tundra do? No matter how she felt, she would stand tall, tail high, and offer true leadership as the alpha dog to the rest of the pack, especially if they were downhearted. He sighed, tried to lift his head off his paws, but it was weighted. Heavy with failure. How could he be of any use now in protecting the other sea turtles on the verge of hatching? What good were they as a Dog Watch team if they couldn't keep watch on the beach tonight? He remembered

Dr. Brita's command to bring back "the gold" to her tonight. He knew that, to her, gold meant eggs for her display. Scientific displays or not, Kito couldn't allow that to happen.

"Chico, Chester, and Schmitty," he began, forcing himself to his feet. "We need to come up with a plan of escape."

"Escape? From this cell?" Chico asked. "You've gotta be kidding. No dog escapes from here."

"Nobody? Don't you have stories of dogs who somehow got out of here? Maybe they found a chink in the wall, and dug and dug and dug. . . ."

Chico walked the short perimeter of the room. He looked at the corners and floor as he did so, then stood beside Kito. "There are no chinks. The cement of this building is thick and built to last."

"Then what about through those bars on the window?"

As Chico walked over to the steel bars, an iguana crawled off the outside window ledge and up into the nearby branches. Kito

had seen a few since they'd arrived and marveled at how they blended in—and startled him when they moved!

Chico pushed his nose between two bars. "Look," he said. "I have the smallest head of all of you. And I can't slip through. Maybe a Chihuahua slipped through these bars once in the past. Maybe. But I have never heard such a story. But us? It's not going to happen."

Kito tried to think harder. "But there has to be a way out! We can't just wait until someone decides to let us go. That could be days, months, years! We must brainstorm for an action plan."

"Well, *amigo*," Chico said, "there is one way of escape."

"Then why didn't you say so?"

"Because, well, because it's so simple that I didn't think you'd want to hear it. You were looking for something grand, I think. This is not."

"Please," Kito said. "Tell us."

All the dogs turned their attention to

Chico, who sat down in the middle of the cell. *"Amigos,* when somebody decides to turn the key in that door, then that's when we escape."

Kito began pacing. "But who knows when that will be! We have to get out by nightfall so we can guard the nests. You all heard what I heard at the Eco Center."

"Then by nightfall it is," Chico replied.

"What?" Kito sat on his rump. "What do you mean?"

"At sundown, Fernando the jailer always comes to feed whatever dogs are in the cell."

"Sí," said the toothless dog in the corner, apparently able to understand English.

"And he puts water in with Julio's dog food because he knows he has a hard time chewing. He lets it soften up. He's kind that way."

"Sí," Julio agreed.

"And so," Chico said. "When the jailer steps in to feed us, he'll give Julio his food first. He'll expect that we'll wait for him to come back with our food, which any dog would do when it never knows where its next meal is coming from. But we, well, we all have homes. So we could risk escape at that moment when the door is ajar. We'll just run out before he gets back. Easy, *sí*?"

Chester jumped up. "Now you're thinking! Hearty Hound, here I come!"

The talk turned to favorite dog foods and dinnertime. Kito couldn't believe how hard it was sometimes to keep dogs focused on a mission when food was in the air. He would rather skip dinner completely and head straight for the beach than stop by the condo. By doing so, they risked getting locked inside for the rest of the night.

But they were a team. And he was outnumbered.

One way or another, they had to stick together.

Just as Chico had predicted, and just as the sun touched the western sky's edge, a key turned in the cell door.

"*Buenas noches, amigos!*" A man stepped

in carrying a bowl in front of his round belly. He delivered the dog food bowl to toothless Julio and set it gently before the aging canine. The man knelt beside the dog and scratched his ears while Julio ate, wagging his tail in gratitude.

"Let's go!" Chico announced.

The dogs—all except Julio—darted out the door and into the cooling shadows of evening.

They raced past several restaurants, where workers set outdoor tables with tablecloths, vases of hibiscus flowers, and candles.

"Full moon tonight," Kito said, noting the bright sphere rising over the bay. "Dinner, some normal time with our owners, and then we meet back at the beach. Okay with you, Chico?" He felt the need to defer to Chico since he himself was just a visitor and Chico lived here.

"*Sí, amigo.* A very good plan."

Full Moon Rising

The dogs stopped by the back steps of a house and found a dish of dog food waiting. "This is my home," Chico said. "My food, too." He barked twice, but Juan didn't appear. So Chico gulped down his food and trotted off again toward the beach with Kito, Chester, and Schmitty.

As the dogs approached the condo, Mrs. H and Hillary looked up from their magazines at the poolside table. "Well, look who made it home for dinner!" said Mrs. H.

"And Chico came to visit too," Hillary added with a smile.

After the dogs ate—Chico was offered a bowl of food too—they stretched out near the pool. The Hollinghorsts and Hillary settled into a game of cards at the patio table.

"I was a little nervous," Mrs. H said, examining her cards, "about bringing the dogs on this trip. But it's working out just fine, isn't it?"

"Seems to be," Hillary replied. She slapped down her cards. "All jacks," she said.

The four dogs rested near the table waiting for the right time to sneak off down the beach. Kito had advised they linger in case their owners had anything valuable to chat about. Time passed, and finally Mr. H said, "Wasn't it simply wonderful to watch so many turtle nests hatch today?"

Kito's ears perked up, but his heart sank at the same time. He'd missed so much in the jail cell! If only those *strangers* hadn't ruined everything. The dogs had only been trying to help the turtles. He closed his eyes. He loved being almost nose to nose with the tiny creatures. He could have spent the whole afternoon watching each turtle make its trek across the sand. He would have made sure each one made its journey safely. Now, how was he to know? What if a pelican had dove down and caught one as it reached the water? If he'd been there, he could have barked and chased any predators away. What if a child tried to take one home as a pet? He could have prevented that, too, with just a little growling. Now he'd never know for sure.

"With so many people watching," Hillary said, "I think every baby turtle made it to the water. Only nest number three is left."

Only one nest left? Kito was stunned. They'd missed *many* nests hatching on the same day?

"And thank goodness we were there to help with nest number seven," Mrs. H said. "Everyone thought they had all hatched, but then there was the faintest stirring of sand. I just knew something was down there, trying to get out. Must have been buried deeper than all the other eggs."

"Good work, honey," Mr. H said, putting his hand on his wife's shoulder. "You helped give birth today."

Mrs. H laughed, played a card, and said. "Looks like I won!"

When darkness was growing, Kito stretched and rose, and the other dogs did the same. They ambled off toward the beach. Already, hermit crabs were headed in the same direction, scritch-scratching across the sand, carrying their homes of various sizes and colors on their backs.

Kito was lost in thought. He had an idea where nest number three was. Maybe he hadn't made a difference protecting the other nests, but this last nest needed his help. With Dr. Brita and her gang out to collect specimens for their display, this last nest was their last chance. The research students would have to raid it if they didn't want to get sent back home. And Kito was determined not to let that happen.

"C'mon, gang," he said, trotting to the left along the beach. "They mentioned a last nest, and I think I saw a sign—"

"*Hombre,*" Chico said, his voice carrying a hint of awe. "You can read?"

"Ah, no, I was just saying . . ."

"*Sí,* you were saying you saw a sign. But signs have squiggles on them that people can decipher. Not dogs. Tell me true. Can you read?"

Kito realized that Chester and Schmitty were out of listening range. They were trailing behind, distracted by scraps of picnic remains.

"You want the truth?" Kito asked.

"*Sí, Señore.* Always the truth. Haven't you heard 'the truth shall set you free'?"

Kito wondered if he'd feel better if another dog in the world knew he could read. What harm could come of it if Chico learned of his skill? Maybe he would feel less burdened by sharing his secret. He sighed. "Yes, it's true. I can read."

"But this is incredible!" Chico cried out. "A dog who can read!"

"Shhhh," Kito said. "You must promise. This is our secret, please."

Suddenly Chester and Schmitty bounded across the sand. "What is this? A dog can read?" Schmitty asked. "This is big! Huge! It could make all the difference in the world of dogs!"

"Who is it?" Schmitty asked. "What dog here in Mexico can read? If this is true, dogs could start going to school to learn to read. They could learn to read books!"

"Drive cars!" Chester added.

"Drive cars?" Kito repeated, his head cocked.

"Oh, well, criminy, maybe not drive cars. But we could read maps. Point with our paws to where we want to go. We could do more stuff, that's all. So who *is* this dog?"

Chico sniffed. "A legend of Mexico," he said. "A wish that lies in the heart of every dog. To learn to read and to read well."

"Such a noble dream." Chester sat down heavily in the sand with a sigh. "It makes me wonder if such a dream is possible. But all dreams start with wishes. . . ."

The dogs trotted along the beach until Kito spotted the sign he'd been looking for. Fortunately, the sign was illuminated under the moon's white beam. He read it to himself: "Nest number three." That was the last nest to hatch. The one they had to protect at all costs.

He pretended to sniff around and find it with his nose. "Hey, I think this nest is still active. I think I can smell baby turtles in the sand, waiting to hatch."

"I thought I had a good nose," Chester said,

"but you're proving to almost be a match for my royal beagle skills. Good work, Kito!"

"Thanks." Kito dropped down to rest in the sand. "Now, let's settle in and keep watch. As the moon rises higher, we'll be able to see anyone—friend or foe—approach this nest. So what are we going to do to stay awake?"

"Hide!" Chico warned, suddenly in motion, sending sand flying.

Kito jumped to his feet. Chico led the charge to the shrubs and bushes on the higher edge of beach. It was a stretch that had no condos—only jungle beyond.

"Quick!" Chico called. "Someone's coming!"

12

Lying in Wait

Palm branches rustled overhead. Flattened to the sand, Kito gazed out. A few clouds blew clear, and the moon aimed its beam directly on nest number three. Beneath the sand, several yards away from where they hid, baby sea turtles, Kito knew, waited in their shells for the right time to peck free.

"It's not that we don't believe you, Chico," Kito said, "but it's just, well—" He looked to the left, then to the right. The beach was empty. The only movement he spotted was the shimmery reflection of moonlight on soft waves. "There's just not anyone in sight, that's all."

"*Hombres*, I heard something," Chico said.

The tuft of hair beneath his new friend's chin reminded Kito of a small beard.

"Thing is," Chico said, "you might be looking for something on two legs, when maybe what I heard doesn't have any legs at all."

"Dancing dalmatians!" Chester cried. "No legs at all? What are you trying to do, get us so scared we have to run home?"

"Oh, I see what he means," Schmitty said. "Something otherworldly. Like aliens! Maybe a UFO landed nearby!"

"Sorry, bud," Chester said, "but we would have spotted a UFO on a night like this. I don't think so."

"Maybe," Schmitty continued, "Chico means something with no legs . . . something like a ghost. Is that it, Chico?"

Kito shivered. He didn't believe in UFOs, but ghosts . . . well, he didn't know what he thought about ghosts. All he knew was he had no desire to go looking for them. He thought of the skeleton in the village, sitting on display in a chair. So strange. He couldn't imagine people in Pembrook using skeletons for decorations unless it was at Halloween. With so many skeletons around, maybe ghosts were wandering around Mexico too! The wind rattled the palm branches a little harder, as if in agreement. Kito tried to stop thinking. He was spooking himself silly.

Chico finally spoke up. "No, *amigos*. I don't mean ghosts. I'm not saying that one couldn't be out there, but really, what would a ghost want with sea turtle eggs?"

"You've got a point," Chester replied. "So, something with no legs, something that's not a ghost—"

"I still think it could be an alien," Schmitty said. "Come to think of it, most aliens I've seen on TV usually have two legs."

Chico seemed to be enjoying the suspense. He sat up, stood to his short shaggy legs, and walked back and forth between the other dogs, who were all lying flat against the sand. "Snakes," Chico said matter-of-factly.

"Barkin' biscuits!" Chester cried out, popping up and running in circles. "Where?"

"I'm just saying," Chico went on, "that's what I *might* have heard. After all, snakes have to eat, don't they?"

"Oh," Schmitty said. "Like eggs of baby sea turtles?"

Kito thought of the common garter snake in Minnesota. It wasn't all that scary.

"*Amigos,*" Chico said, "if you left the roadway past your condo and went into the jungle, I tell you, you'd find some snakes big enough to eat *you.*"

"What kind of snake is that big?" Schmitty asked.

"The boa constrictor, *amigo.*"

"For the love of the queen of England!" Chester yelped. He glanced inland toward the jungle. "Suddenly I don't care all that much about turtle eggs! It's my own hide I'm thinking about!"

"Me too!" Schmitty called out. "I'm outta here!"

The two touched noses and then raced toward the edge of the water and straight home—to their owners.

Chico studied Kito. "And what about you? Aren't you afraid of snakes?"

"Big ones like you mentioned," Kito said. "Of course."

"Then why didn't you run away too?"

"I, well, I made a promise—"

"What kind of promise?"

"It's hard to put into words," Kito said, shivering under his warm fur but standing firm. Moonlight flooded the bay and illuminated the last marked nest.

"Well, a promise is a promise," Chico said. "And if you made a promise to watch over this nest, then I will join you in this noble cause. Snake or no snake, you and I, we will stay. *Sí*?"

"*Sí*," Kito replied. Without explaining, Chico had understood. He was a real friend. Kito figured it wouldn't hurt to try out the little bit of Spanish he was picking up as well. *"Sí, amigo. Gracias."*

Gradually, the moon helped ease Kito's fears. He let out a breath and felt the tension go from his tight shoulders. He watched the beach for anyone approaching. He gazed out at the sea, hoping to catch a glimpse of an adult sea turtle as it lifted its head. He soaked in the steady coming and going of waves, as if the ocean itself were breathing. It was a perfect night, one he wouldn't miss for the world. If he was lucky, he'd be around when the last nest hatched.

If all went well, he would stay awake and they would have no unexpected visitors in the night.

13

Keeping Watch

Kito woke up, certain that he was back at home with Chester snoring at the end of the Hollinghorsts' bed. But whistling wind and crashing waves brought him to his senses. It was Chico who was snoring. And he, who had vowed to stay awake and keep an eye on the nest, had fallen asleep!

"Chico, wake up!" Kito said.

The moon had disappeared behind clouds and the night gathered around them as ominous as ghosts. "I can barely see the nest," Kito complained. "What if something—or someone—has raided it?" He rose to stiff legs, stretched, then trotted down the sloping sand to the little flag. He sniffed around, but smelled nothing new. And then, his back hairs shot up at attention. He heard voices.

Chico rushed to his side. "*Amigo*, we know those voices."

"Sure do," Kito replied. The dogs stood shoulder to shoulder, waiting in the darkness, guarding the nest. A flashlight beam switched on, then traveled back and forth in long arcing motions across the beach.

"I just don't like the idea of taking eggs." It was the girl from the Eco Center. Kaitlyn. "Something about the way Dr. Brita is acting doesn't feel right."

"We're just research students," Jenks replied in his twangy, whiny voice.

The footsteps and voices came closer until the beam of light fell directly on the two dogs. Kito blinked up at the light, completely blinded.

"What on earth?" Jenks exclaimed.

"Hey, we saw these dogs earlier some-where. Must be beach dogs. Hey, fellas. We're not going to hurt you."

Kito growled, then Chico joined in.

"Settle down, dogs. Now get away from the nest."

Kito wasn't going to be driven away, even if the voices were friendly. He knew what their intention was: to raid the nest so the eggs could be used for a science display. He couldn't let that happen.

"Be careful," Kaitlyn said. "You don't want to get bit."

"Well, I can't go back empty-handed," Jenks whined. "You heard her. And I need the credits for this program in order to grad-uate on time. So do you. Plus, my parents will kill me if I have to go another semester! I mean, college isn't cheap!"

"Tell me about it," Kaitlyn replied. "But still, the way she's sending us out in the middle of the night to gather eggs. I mean, it feels wrong. Like maybe she really doesn't have the permit. I mean, it's like she's sending us to do something criminal."

"Yeah, if we took eggs in the middle of broad daylight, I suppose locals and tourists would get pretty angry."

"Huh," Kaitlyn shot back. "You think?"

Kaitlyn and Jenks moved closer, then stopped.

Kito braced himself, all four legs planted squarely in the sand.

"It's as if they're guarding the nest," said Jenks, gazing down at the dogs.

"Huh, guarding their potential next meal," added Kaitlyn. "The question is, how do we get them away from the nest?"

Kito turned his growls to barking, then pretended to lunge toward their legs, as if to bite them. Of course, he wouldn't bite them, but he certainly wanted to give them a good scare.

"Watch out!" Jenks cried.

"Hey, maybe kick sand in their eyes."

At that, Chico called out, *"Amigo!* Charge!" As one, before the students could as much as draw back a leg to kick sand, the dogs charged them and sent the students fleeing. Kito and Chico yipped and snarled, raced and growled. They herded the students down the beach, darting in and out between them, keeping them moving away from the nest. When they neared a cluster of villas, Kaitlyn and Jenks ran toward safety.

Kito and Chico stopped, their feet in the wet sand, and watched the students disappear.

"I could use a sip of water," Kito said, his chest heaving. He stepped toward the waves.

"Not that water, *amigo*."

"Oh, I forgot."

Chico led Kito to the nearest outdoor pool. Heads down, they lapped up a slightly chlorinated drink. But it was better than salt water.

The night darkness began to fade to purplish gray. "Hey, it's almost morning," Kito said. "Looks like we managed to protect the nest through the night. I feel good about that. Thanks for your help, Chico."

"*No problemo, amigo.*"

"No problem?" Kito said.

"*Sí, no problemo.*"

Head high, Kito trotted back with Chico toward the nest. As they worked their way around what the tide had left behind—a plastic bottle cap, a child's flip-flop, a long timber, chunks of coral, and seashells—Kito kept an eye on the ocean. Maybe, just maybe, he'd spot a sea turtle.

When they arrived at nest number three, Kito's heart dropped to his paws. The nest was stirred up, as if someone had been exploring it with a stick. On the surface, the remains of one shell lay broken in bits, without any evidence of a hatching. Kito sniffed around and frantically searched through loose sand. "No! This is terrible!"

"Maybe it hatched," Chico said, sniffing the broken shell. "But just as it came out of its shell, something ate it."

Out of the corner of his eye, Kito spotted movement higher on the beach, followed by a rustle and a whoosh between bushes, and then something shot up the nearest palm tree.

"Up there!" Kito said. His senses told him that they had caught the intruder, though what it was, he still couldn't tell. It had to be a boa constrictor—something fast moving, dangerous, and deadly.

"Chico! Start barking! We need all the help we can get!"

Kito yelped and barked all at once. Then he turned his bark up to full volume, as if lives depended on him, which was true! He welled up all his determination—the full force of Dog Watch in his voice. He barked with the full depth of Gunnar's bellow; he barked with the courage of Tundra; he barked with the energy of Muffin; he barked with the heart of Lucky. He barked and barked and barked until he heard Chester and Schmitty in the distance, joining in, racing down the beach in his direction. As they came up beside him, the sun broke across the horizon, as if to help spotlight the intruder.

14

Caught!

With the day's first light, Kito ran to a palm tree, looked up, and spotted the culprit. He couldn't quite believe his eyes. He'd expected a giant snake, or maybe an iguana of gigantic size. Instead, a furry striped brown creature looked down at him. With its hind feet and one front hand it held on to the trunk of the tree. In its other little hand it held a baby sea turtle by its tail, dangling it high in the air.

"A raccoon?" Kito called out. "Here? In Mexico?" He'd seen them at home plenty

of times, but they were the last animal he expected to see here on the beach.

"*Sí*, Kito," Chico answered. "I didn't think they would go after turtles. It was probably hoping to find a yolk, not a live turtle."

"Will it eat the turtle?" Kito asked with dread.

"I don't know, *Señore*."

At that, Kito barked all the more loudly. He jumped up and down at the base of the palm tree, hoping to scare the raccoon into dropping the baby turtle to the sand. Getting dropped might be bad, but getting eaten would be far worse!

"Hey, what'cha got there?" Schmitty called, coming up alongside Kito.

"Look up, you'll see!"

"What's shaking?" Chester asked, racing in to join the dogs.

"I wish we could shake this raccoon out of the tree!"

No sooner had the dogs joined up than the two beach rakers who had hauled them off to the local jail arrived. They shook their fists at the dogs and spoke in Spanish.

The dogs danced away from the men. "We can't get caught again!" Kito shouted. "Stay lively! Dart and move!"

Suddenly, one of the beach rakers looked up at the palm tree. He pointed. *"Tortuga!"*

"Is that Spanish for 'raccoon'?" Kito asked Chico. The dogs stopped moving and watched the beach rakers.

"No, *hombre. Tortuga* means 'turtle'! He's worried too, about the baby turtle!"

The beach rakers shifted their concern from the dogs to the raccoon, who peered down at everyone with its black mask. A bandit, caught in the act of nest raiding!

When one of the men picked up a hardened chunk of beach coral, Kito flinched. He didn't know if the man intended to pelt the dogs or the raccoon. Kito had hoped to chase off the raccoon, not kill it. Then the man wound up and threw the coral so that it struck just inches above the raccoon's grip on the tree, enough to startle it into dropping the baby sea turtle, which fell to the sand and remained motionless. And all in one flash of movement, the raccoon (while the beach rakers turned their attention toward the turtle), pushed off from the trunk of the palm tree, landed yards away on the ground, and disappeared between the fronds of bushes and into the jungle beyond.

The two men approached the sea turtle.

"Stay back a bit," Kito advised. "We don't want to be hauled off again. If we show we're respectful . . ."

The older man squatted to the baby turtle and picked it up in his hand. He spoke softly, encouragingly, in words that Kito didn't understand. But he knew what the man was probably saying, anyway. Something like what he would have said: "C'mon, little turtle. Little *tortuga*. You can make it! Don't die!"

At long last a little head emerged from its shell. It stretched the thin skin on its green neck and looked around at the world. Its eyes were wide open and ready. *"Bueno!"* The man's eyes filled with tears. *"Bueno!"*

Then the man walked with the turtle back to nest number three. He set the turtle in the sand, right beside the remains of its shell. The dogs clustered around, but with enough distance so as not to cause alarm.

Then the sea turtle started to move. With a paddling motion, it pushed back grains of sand, swished its little tail across the sand, and crawled straight for the water. As it did, a group of approaching walkers neared.

"Oh, no," Kito said, fearing that they'd shoo the dogs away, just like they had yesterday. But it wasn't a strange group of tourists. It was Mr. and Mrs. H, Hillary Rothchild, Carlos, the manager, and Juan, the jewelry seller.

"Tortugas!" Juan called out.

They came closer, just as the baby turtle reached the water, paddled out onto the first wave, then dove beneath and headed out to sea.

"Kito!" Mrs. H said, falling to her knees beside him. She wrapped her arms around his neck. "We didn't know what had happened to you! Then we heard barking and knew it had to be you. I thought something was attacking you!"

The beach rakers spoke in Spanish to Carlos, pointing up at the tree, then toward the jungle beyond.

"Your dogs helped save a sea turtle," Carlos explained to the others. "A raccoon had been up to no good."

"Well, isn't that something?" Mr. H said with a shake of his head. He patted Kito's head. "Is that true?"

Hillary looked at Schmitty. "I've always said they're smarter than we know," she said with a smile. "We thought they were just running around having fun, and here they were keeping the world safe." She chuckled to herself. "Here they were out keeping the world safe for sea turtles."

Kito had to smile to himself. He glanced at the waiting nest. They didn't know the half of it! And at that, as if to join the early morning gathering, nest number three began to stir. It was so faint at first that Kito thought he'd imagined it. Grains of sand stirred and began to move. And before he knew it, another sea turtle, wearing a freshly cracked fleck of eggshell as a hat, pushed its way out of the sand. Kito barked with excitement.

"Look!" Juan cried. *"Tortuga!"*

Everyone gathered around, some standing, some kneeling in the sand. The dogs clustered nearby too, some standing, others flat on their bellies, watching.

Minute by minute, the scene changed. The nest began to unearth itself. One, two, three turtles emerged. Then, with a clear sense of mission and purpose, they pointed their noses toward the ocean and began the journey from sand to water.

Three more people approached the nest. Kito stood on guard. It was Dr. Brita, followed by her research students.

"Hola!" Dr. Brita called out.

They joined in with everyone else, watching the spectacle. Four, five, six turtles emerged. That made seven in total! Kito felt a huge wave of relief roll over him. His promise was nearly fulfilled. And no matter how much Dr. Brita and her research students needed turtle eggs for display, they were too late now. They couldn't do any collecting this season, no matter the purpose.

Kito watched the last turtle slide into the ocean with a sense of satisfaction.

"We should make sure," Dr. Brita said, "that there aren't more trying to hatch. She reached into the pit of sand. She pulled out one round egg, about the size of a golf ball, held it to her ear, and then set it out for everyone to see. And then, reaching deeper, she pulled out another white egg. She held this one to her ear, but for a much longer time. That one too, she set on the sand.

"We must watch and wait," she said, crossing her arms over her chest.

They didn't wait long to see a crack emerge in the first egg. Gradually, as the sun began to warm Kito's back, the turtle's head and right foot broke through, and then, squeezing its webbed foot against the shell, it ripped itself free and crawled out.

Everyone cheered! As they watched it crawl to the water, Kito kept an eye on the other egg. It might be just like Dr. Brita to pocket that last egg when no one was watching. But as the attention returned to the remaining egg, Dr. Brita pointed to it. "We could wait all day for this one," she explained, "and it would never hatch. Not all eggs make it. This one never developed into a healthy turtle."

She passed the egg around, and the people held it to their ears.

"No *vida*," the younger beach raker said.

"What's that?" Kito whispered to Chico.

"*Vida* is 'life,'" Chico said. "No *vida*."

Last to listen to the egg, Hillary handed it back to Dr. Brita, who set it on the ground. Then the dogs all took turns sniffing the egg.

"Nope," Schmitty said.

"No life," Chico concluded.

"The smell of death," Chester said sadly.

Kito didn't put his nose to the egg. He held back.

"Aren't you going to sniff the egg, Kito?" Schmitty asked.

"No," he said, "I trust you guys." He didn't want his last encounter with sea turtles to end that way. No, he'd rather think on all the sea turtles that made it to the sea, including the one they had helped rescue from the raccoon. His mission was accomplished. *Their* mission was accomplished. He glanced at the waves. A dip would feel good. He shook off his coat, ready to get going.

"If you all don't mind," Dr. Brita said, picking up the egg and holding it carefully in the palm of her hand, "we would like to add this egg to our research collection for display purposes."

Everyone nodded or voiced agreement, and the research students elbowed one another.

"Gather nest signs," the doctor commanded the students. "Chart the hatching time, the number of successful eggs in nest number three. You know the drill."

Kaitlyn promptly pulled out a clipboard

from her backpack and began writing. As Jenks yanked the flag from the sand, he whooped. "Hey, now we won't be sent home early!"

Kito looked to Schmitty, Chester, and Chico. "Dare you!" he said.

And without another word, the dogs gave chase. Kito twisted and turned. He darted in and out between the fast-moving legs of his canine friends. They whipped up tiny sandstorms across the beach as they ran ahead of their owners, who strolled down the beach at a lazy pace.

When the three dogs were hot on his tail, Kito turned a sharp left into the waves. The ocean cooled his underbelly, soaked his thick coat until it clung like a shaggy, wet jacket. His canine friends joined him, jumping in and out as the water rushed back toward the ocean. The next thing Kito knew, a wave tumbled them all head over heels. Kito spun in the water, then surfaced, and the next wave dropped him onshore. He rested on the wet sand, catching his breath.

Chester called out. "For the love of *tortugas*! That was awesome!"

Kito had to agree. All was well in this Mexican village. The sea turtle eggs at Half Moon Bay had all hatched. He'd lived up to his secret promise. In a few short days he'd be back on Dog Watch duty in Pembrook. It was time to make the most of his vacation. He stretched and rose to his legs.

"C'mon, Kito!" Schmitty called.

"Come in, *amigo*!" Chico added. "The water's great!"

A foamy wave rushed up and tickled Kito's paws. It had been a long night. A good, long nap in the shade was just what he needed—*after* one more good tumble in the waves!

He plunged in.

The Newbery Medal is awarded each year to the most distinguished contribution to literature for children published in the U.S. How many of these honor books, available from Aladdin Paperbacks, have you read?

NEWBERY HONOR BOOKS

❑ *The Bears on Hemlock Mountain*
by Alice Dalgliesh
0-689-71604-4

❑ *Misty of Chincoteague*
by Marguerite Henry
1-4169-2789-2

❑ *Calico Bush*
by Rachel Field
0-689-82285-5

❑ *The Courage of Sarah Noble*
by Alice Dalgliesh
0-689-71540-4

❑ *The Dark Is Rising*
by Susan Cooper
0-689-71087-9

❑ *Dogsong*
by Gary Paulsen
0-689-80409-1

❑ *The Golden Fleece*
by Padraic Colum
0-689-86884-7

❑ *The Moorchild*
by Eloise McGraw
0-689-82033-X

❑ *Hatchet*
by Gary Paulsen
1-4169-3647-5

❑ *The Jazz Man*
by Mary Hays Weik
0-689-71767-9

❑ *Justin Morgan Had a Horse*
by Marguerite Henry
1-4169-2785-9

❑ *The Planet of Junior Brown*
by Virginia Hamilton
1-4169-1410-2

❑ *A String in the Harp*
by Nancy Bond
1-4169-2771-9

❑ *Sugaring Time*
by Kathryn Lasky
0-689-71081-X

❑ *Volcano*
by Patricia Lauber
0-689-71679-6

❑ *Yolonda's Genius*
by Carol Fenner
0-689-81327-9